D1486710

Jennifer Jean, the Cross-Eyed Queen

by Phyllis Reynolds Naylor

illustrated by Karen Ritz

916269

Carolrhoda Books, Inc./Minneapolis

To Mother and all her pupils—P.R.N.

To Kate—K.R.

This edition first published 1994 by Carolrhoda Books, Inc.

Illustrations copyright © 1994 by Carolrhoda Books, Inc.
Text copyright © 1967 by Lerner Publications.

Carolrhoda Books, Inc. c/o The Lerner Group
241 First Avenue North, Minneapolis, MN 55401

Library of Congress Cataloging-in-Publication Data

Naylor, Phyllis Reynolds.
    Jennifer Jean, the Cross-Eyed Queen / Phyllis Reynolds Naylor : with
illustrations by Karen Ritz.
        p.   cm.
    Summary: Jennifer Jean likes her big green crossed eyes and does not want
them changed, but when she goes to kindergarten in September she is a
little bit glad that they were straightened.
    ISBN 0-87614-791-0 (lib. bdg.)
    [1. Eye–Diseases and defects–Fiction.] I. Ritz, Karen, ill. II. Title.
PZ7.N24Je 1994
[E]–dc20   93-4100
                                                                  CIP
                                                                  AC

Manufactured in the United States of America

1 2 3 4 5 6 – P/JR – 99 98 97 96 95 94

Jennifer Jean was born with two big eyes, just like everybody else. Sometimes when Mother looked at them she said, "I think these eyes are going to be blue." And Father would say, "I think they are going to be brown."

But as the little baby grew bigger, her eyes became green—as green as the grass and the leaves and her mother's best hat. Everyone said, "What beautiful eyes she has! What beautiful green eyes!"

As Jennifer Jean grew older, she began to walk and talk and jump.
Then she began to squint. She wrinkled her forehead up, so that no
one could see her green eyes at all, and tipped her head to one side.
Mother and Father thought it was very strange. One day they noticed
something even stranger. Jennifer Jean's eyes were crossed. One eye
looked one way and one looked another.

Jennifer Jean grew bigger. She learned to skip rope. She learned to hang upside down by her knees on the monkey bars. And she could sing all three verses of "Way Down Yonder in the Paw Paw Patch." Her hair grew longer and her hands got bigger. But her eyes stayed crossed. Nobody said, "What beautiful green eyes she has!" anymore, and sometimes people turned and looked the other way.

One day when Jennifer Jean was four years old, Mother said, "Soon we are going to see the doctor about your eyes. Wouldn't it be nice to have them straight again?"

But Jennifer Jean was not sure. None of her playmates had crossed eyes. None of the other children could see their noses as well as she could see hers. Sometimes she just liked to sit and look at it.

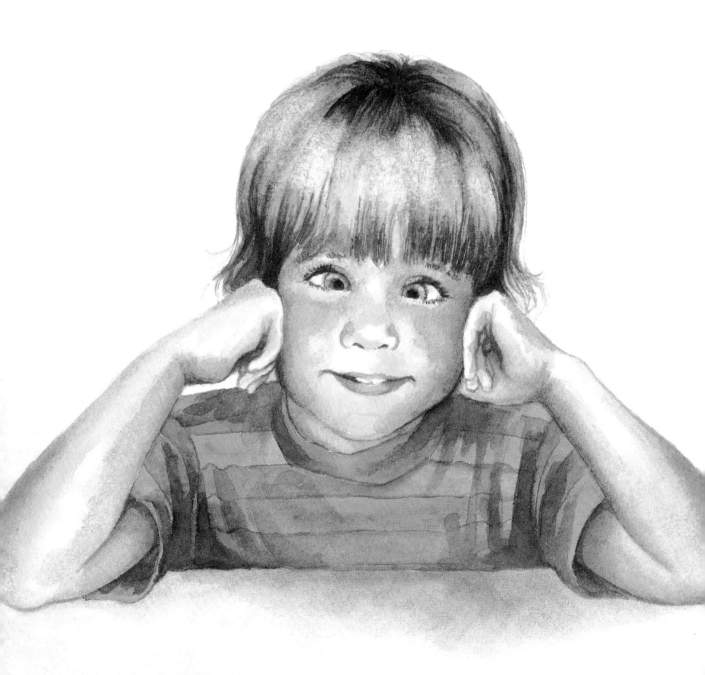

The boys teased her. "Jennifer Jean, Cross-Eyed Queen!" And Jennifer Jean yelled right back, "I'm Jennifer Jean, the Cross-Eyed Queen, and if I blink my eyes three times you'll turn into a toad." The boys would be quiet for a while in case she meant it.

"Jennifer Jean—her eyes look mean," the girls chanted. And Jennifer Jean growled like a tiger and showed her claws and chased them all away.

Little John Stone Lewis made up a song:

"Jennifer Jean, Cross-Eyed Queen,
Must have got hit by the kitchen screen."

When he sang it to her, Jennifer Jean put a paper sack over her head and said she was turning into a witch underneath. John Stone Lewis promised not to tease her again if she would take it off, and she did.

But Big Butch Edwards didn't tease Jennifer Jean. When he saw her playing all alone, he came over and sat in the swing.

"My eyes used to be crossed, too," he said.

Jennifer Jean was building a sand fort. She didn't say a word.

"I didn't like my eyes that way," said Butch.

Jennifer Jean went on building her fort. She put guns on the towers and guards at the doors.

"The doctor made my eyes straight," said Butch, "and I'm glad he did."

Jennifer Jean stood up and walked on her sand fort, knocking it all down. "Mother says I am going to have my eyes straightened too, but I like them the way they are."

"You'll like them more later," insisted Butch. "You don't want to be different from everybody else, do you?"

Jennifer Jean was different. None of the other children squinted their eyes and tipped their heads. None of the other children stumbled over toys the way Jennifer Jean seemed to do. And there were things that the other children could do that Jennifer Jean couldn't do well at all, such as stringing beads and cutting out paper dolls.

"What's wrong with being different?" Jennifer Jean asked her mother.

"Nothing," said Mother. "If everybody looked and acted the same, I wouldn't be able to tell you from Butch or Susie or John Stone Lewis."

Jennifer Jean giggled. "But we're all different. John Stone Lewis has ears that stick out and Susie has big feet and I have crossed eyes."

"Yes," said Mother. "But sometimes, if the difference causes trouble, it's good to do something about it. I think you would see a lot better if your eyes were straight."

"Huh uh," said Jennifer Jean. "I can see fine." And she bumped into a chair.

One day Jennifer Jean said to the grocer, "I am going to the doctor Saturday. She is going to make my eyes straight."

The grocer seemed surprised. He leaned way over the counter and looked at Jennifer Jean. "Why, I had forgotten they were crossed," he said. "There are so many other things to look at—fingers and freckles and such." He winked and stuck a piece of peppermint in Jennifer Jean's pocket.

Jennifer Jean told John Stone Lewis that she was going to get her eyes straightened.

"Good," said John.

Jennifer Jean told her cat that she was going to have her eyes straightened. The cat didn't even know her eyes were crossed. He just knew that Jennifer Jean's lap was soft.

On Saturday Mother and Jennifer Jean went to the eye doctor. Jennifer Jean kept her eyes closed all the way. Mother had to lead her up the stairs.

"Open your eyes," Mother said. "Stop being silly."

Jennifer Jean bumped into a big man with a briefcase. The man said, "Ooof!" and hurried away. Jennifer Jean opened her eyes and kept them open.

"We're going to do something about those eyes," said the doctor.

"I don't want you to do anything about my eyes," Jennifer Jean insisted. "I have beautiful eyes."

"Yes you do," said the doctor. "Beautiful green eyes. And I will try to make them even prettier."

She gave Jennifer Jean a present. It was a little black patch on a string. The doctor put the patch over one of Jennifer Jean's eyes and slipped the string around her head.

She looked like a pirate.

But it was no fun at all, for everything looked blurred and fuzzy—the door, the doctor, the pictures on the walls, and even her mother's green hat.

Just when Jennifer Jean was about to say, "I won't wear it," she heard the doctor tell her mother that she was to get glasses right away.

"In a few days, your eyes will feel much better and things won't look so fuzzy," the doctor said. "Best of all, after you have worn the eye patch and the glasses for a while, your eyes will begin to get straighter. You'll see."

Jennifer Jean was very quiet as she and her mother rode home.
"What's the matter, Jennifer Jean?" Mother asked.
"I'm not Jennifer Jean," said Jennifer Jean. "I am a pirate. I am thinking about my ship."
"Oh," said Mother.

When Jennifer Jean got home, she heard her friends calling her from the backyard. She went to the door, but the steps looked all tippy and steep. When she tried to walk down them, she slipped and tumbled right to the bottom.

The children came over and stared at her. Susie Salez put her hands over her mouth. "Oh, Jennifer Jean, you look so funny!" she giggled.

And John Stone Lewis said,

"Jennifer Jean, the Cross-Eyed Queen,
Fell down the steps and broke her bean."

Jennifer Jean slowly got to her feet. "I'm Jennifer Jean, the Pirate Queen," she said. "You'd fall too if you had a wooden leg."

Susie's and John Stone Lewis's mouths opened wide, and Jennifer Jean climbed in the sandbox. "This is my ship," she said.

"I want to be a pirate," said John Stone Lewis. "I've got a wooden leg, too."

"So do I," said Susie.

They all climbed in the sandbox-ship. Every time Jennifer Jean stood up, the children saluted. And when a storm came and the ship was wrecked and everybody fell over the side, Jennifer Jean almost lost her eye patch. She and Susie and John Stone Lewis lay in a heap on the ground and giggled.

"Let me wear the patch a while," John Stone Lewis begged. But when Jennifer Jean started to take it off, Mother called, "Jennifer Jean! You must wear it all the time, you know."

At dinnertime that night, Father called her Pirate Jenny and gave her a treasure. It was a pirate ring. She wore it all evening long and marched around the house with her patch over one eye and her cat on her shoulder.

It was fun being a pirate. Just as the doctor said, she began to see better and better, and soon the patch did not bother her much at all. Then Jennifer Jean and Mother went to get her glasses. They were very pretty and sparkly with green frames to match her eyes. But when Jennifer Jean put them on, she could hardly see again because everything looked so fuzzy. Her head felt dizzy and the room felt tippy and two big tears rolled out from underneath the black eye patch.

"Don't worry," said the man who had polished her glasses. "You will get used to them soon. In a few days, you'll see better than ever before."

This time, when Jennifer Jean got home and went out in the backyard, a lot of boys and girls were playing in the sandbox. When they saw Jennifer Jean with the eye patch over one eye and the glasses on top of that, they began to laugh and hoot and point their fingers. Jennifer Jean could not even tell who they were because their faces looked all fuzzy.

Someone yelled,
    "See her now, cross-eyed gal,
    Big-eyed, one-eyed, black-eyed owl."

But this time, John Stone Lewis did not laugh. He had a secret, and he came over and whispered it in Jennifer Jean's ear.

"Tomorrow," he told her, "I am going to have my ears fixed so they don't stick out. Daddy said so."

"You'll still be the same boy and they'll be the same ears," said Jennifer Jean.

"Of course," said John Stone Lewis, and suddenly that seemed awfully funny. He and Jennifer Jean laughed and laughed. The other children wanted to hear the secret, but Jennifer Jean and John wouldn't tell.

The weeks went by, and Jennifer Jean's eyes grew stronger and stronger. Halloween came. Jennifer Jean scared the stuffing out of everybody by dressing up in pirate's clothes with her black eye patch and tapping on windows with a wooden sword. John Stone Lewis put on floppy rubber ears and rubber teeth and a rubber nose, and every time he opened his mouth, his teeth fell out. Susie Salez dressed up like a fairy princess and looked very pretty in spite of the big feet that she was always going to have.

One day Jennifer Jean did not have to wear the black eye patch anymore. She gave it to her cat. When she pulled it along the floor, the cat ran after it. He thought it was a bug. Once she even put the patch over the cat's head, and he looked like a pirate. She called him Captain Kidd Cat.

Jennifer Jean's eyes were getting straighter. Sometimes they looked as though they weren't crossed at all. But they were. Just a little. The next time Mother and Jennifer Jean went to the doctor, she showed them some exercises to do.

"Twenty times a day," she said, smiling. "Twenty times a day, every single day, and maybe—just maybe—by the time you go to school in September, your eyes will be perfectly straight."

Jennifer Jean wriggled in her chair. "Will my eyes ever go crossed again after we get them straight?" she wanted to know.

"I don't think so," said the doctor. "Not very many children have crossed eyes, but when eyes do cross, it is usually when they are two or three years old. Once your eyes are really, truly straight, I think they will stay that way."

Jennifer Jean worked hard on her exercises. Sometimes she did them thirty times a day. Sometimes she did them in bed in the morning when the birds were just waking up and scolding the cat.

One day she looked in the mirror and her eyes were straight. Perfectly straight. She could hardly believe it. She rolled her eyes in toward her nose and then back again. She looked in the mirror. They were still straight. She rolled her eyes to one side and then another. She looked in the mirror. They were still straight. Everyone who looked at her said, "What beautiful eyes she has! What beautiful green eyes!" And if Jennifer Jean had been Captain Kidd Cat, she would have purred, she was so happy.

On the first day of school, she put on a green dress to match her green glasses and her green eyes.

"Will I have to wear glasses much longer, Mother?" she asked.

"I don't know," said Mother. "We'll have to wait and see."

"Well . . . even if I have to wear them a long time, I'm still the same little girl I always was," said Jennifer Jean.

"Yes," Mother smiled. "A very nice little girl."

Jennifer Jean walked to school that morning with John Stone Lewis whose ears were fixed and Susie Salez whose big feet really didn't matter. John went to second grade, Susie went to first grade, and Jennifer went to kindergarten. All day long she cut and pasted and marched and sang. Everybody called her "Jennifer Jean." Nobody added, "Cross-Eyed Queen." And the teacher thought her glasses were very pretty.

That evening Jennifer Jean gave her father a picture she had painted in school and her mother a paper flower.

"What did you learn today, Jennifer Jean?" asked her father.

"Nothing," said Jennifer Jean, turning a somersault on the rug.

"Whom did you play with?" asked Father.

"Everyone," said Jennifer Jean, standing on her head.

"What did the teacher talk about?" asked Father.

"Everything," said Jennifer Jean, spinning around like a top until she was dizzy and had to stop.

Then she said, "You don't have a little cross-eyed girl anymore, Daddy. Aren't you sorry?"

"No," said Daddy. "I have a beautiful girl with beautiful green eyes. Aren't you glad?"

"No," said Jennifer Jean, hugging Captain Kidd Cat. But she was.
Just a little.